NOAH SCAPE

CAN'T STOP REPEATING HIMSELF

Guy Bass

NOAH SCAPE

CAN'T STOP REPEATING HIMSELF

With illustrations by
Steve May

Barrington Stoke

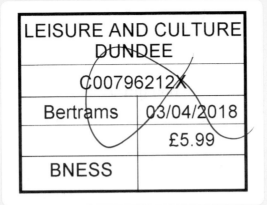
First published in 2018 in Great Britain by
Barrington Stoke Ltd
18 Walker Street, Edinburgh, EH3 7LP

www.barringtonstoke.co.uk

Text © 2018 Guy Bass
Illustrations © 2018 Steve May

A CIP catalogue record for this book is available
from the British Library upon request

ISBN: 978-1-78112-772-8

Printed in China by Leo

CONTENTS

1 Spaghetti and Tomato Sauce...........3

2 Dinosaurs........................9

3 Another Noah 14

4 Noah and the Other Noah 21

5 More Noahs 26

6 Miss Fiddy Faints..................33

7 What a Difference a Weekend Makes ..38

8 You Can't Always Get What You Want...43

9 Enough Is (Not) Enough 48

10 You Might Get What You Need 57

"Welcome to BTVC News. I am Anne Finally, and you join me here, live from the sleepy village of Dundlewick. I was here last month at the start of the so-called 'Dundlewick Doubling'. Today, I look back at how it all began. A month in, the doubling goes on, and on ... and on. Scientists say the number of doubles is set to rise to one billion by tomorrow morning. Today, I examine how the doubling began, and what it means for the future of Dundlewick ... and the human race."

One Month Before ...

Chapter 1
Spaghetti and Tomato Sauce

Dundlewick Doubling – Day Zero
Number Of Noahs – 1

"What's that?" Noah asked. He looked down at the tray of food and screwed up his face.

The dinner lady, Mrs Tuckin, stared back at him.

"Meat pie," she said. Her spatula hovered over the tray, ready to serve him a slice.

"What's in it?" Noah asked.

Mrs Tuckin raised an eyebrow.

"Meat," she said.

"I want spaghetti and tomato sauce," Noah said.

Mrs Tuckin sighed. "And yet here we both are, staring at a tray of meat pie," she replied. "I'll spell it out to you, Noah. I'm sure it won't be for the last time. Monday is spaghetti day. Tuesday is meat pie day. Wednesday is pizza day. Thursday is chicken day. And then, as sure as sugar lumps, it's Friday. And what is Friday otherwise known as?"

"*Fish Friday*," Noah said with a roll of his eyes.

"Fish Friday! From the sea to your plate!" Mrs Tuckin declared.

"Yeah, but –" Noah began.

"But every single day you ask me for spaghetti and tomato sauce," Mrs Tuckin said. "Every. Single. Day."

"That's because I want spaghetti and tomato sauce every day," Noah said in a matter-of-fact way.

"And I want my cat to stop pooing in the fruit bowl," Mrs Tuckin said. "But every day I go home to find that Catilla the Hun has done her business on my satsumas."

"It's like the song says," Mrs Tuckin went on, "'*you can't always get what you want – but, if you try, sometimes you might get what you need ...*'"

"I have no idea what that means," Noah said.

"Give it time," Mrs Tuckin said. "Now, look, Noah, I have a lot of mouths to feed and I know it's hard to believe but they don't all want to eat spaghetti and tomato sauce," she said. Mrs Tuckin pointed to the line of children behind Noah. And, as he looked back at them, she slapped a spatula full of meat pie down on Noah's plate. *"Bon appetit!* Enjoy!" she added. "I look forward to our little chat again tomorrow."

'Why would anyone *not* want to eat spaghetti and tomato sauce?' Noah thought, as he stared down at his plate of meat pie.

If it was up to him, Noah would eat spaghetti and tomato sauce for lunch *and* dinner. He would get up every morning at exactly 06.45 a.m. and go to bed at exactly 10.10 p.m. every night. He would only drink cold milk, and only if it was in a tall glass with a straw. And he would read nothing but books about dinosaurs.

If Noah had his way, everybody else would live by his rules too. But life wasn't like that. Everyone was different. It was *very* frustrating.

'Why can't everyone be like me?' Noah thought. He had to do something about it.

But what?

Chapter 2
Dinosaurs

Noah Scape's day didn't get any better.

How could it? His teacher, Miss Fiddy, was always teaching her class about things like personal pronouns and poisonous plants. She never even mentioned dinosaurs.

Noah knew a *lot* about dinosaurs.

He knew that the dinosaur with the longest name was *Micropachycephalosaurus*.

He knew that the smallest dinosaur egg ever found was only 3 centimetres long.

He knew that the earliest known dinosaur found so far was the *Eoraptor* – and that its skeleton was dug up in Argentina in 1991.

It wasn't just that Noah was interested in dinosaurs – it was that he was interested in nothing else.

But if Noah dared to bring up the differences between the Jurassic and Cretaceous climates in a lesson about poetry, then Miss Fiddy would give him a stern look and say, "No dinosaurs, Noah. Not today."

Noah soon learned that trying to talk about dinosaurs in class was like asking Mrs Tuckin to serve spaghetti and tomato sauce on a Tuesday.

Of course, that didn't mean he stopped trying.

"Now, who can give me an example of a metaphor?" Miss Fiddy asked at 2.59 p.m.

"That is, something that compares one thing to another, without using 'like' or 'as'. Can anyone think of –"

"The *archaeopteryx* was a rainbow of colours!" Noah yelled, waving his hand in the air.

"Well, yes," said Miss Fiddy, trying not to sigh. "I suppose that is a metaphor, but –"

"The *archaeopteryx* is the oldest kind of bird," Noah added, in a loud voice. "The largest kind of *archaeopteryx* could grow to half a metre long, and had a wingspan of –"

"Thank you, Noah," Miss Fiddy said, and she raised her hand. "I think we've heard enough about dinosaurs for one day."

'That makes no sense,' Noah thought. 'How could anyone ever have enough of dinosaurs?'

But it felt like the more Noah cared about dinosaurs, the less everyone else did. All his classmates seemed to care about was playing stupid, pointless, nothing-to-do-with-dinosaurs games, like football or catch or tig.

Even those children who Noah knew *liked* dinosaurs stopped talking about them as soon as he got anywhere near. Instead they chatted about video games and the sizes of planets and why it rains and burping the alphabet and the best colour of socks.

Socks!

'If only,' Noah thought, 'everyone was more like me.' It was the second time that day he'd had that thought. (And the 100th time that year.)

Then Noah decided he would stop wishing '*if only ...*'

Noah decided to *decide*.

So, just as the day was about to end in its usual way – with a loud bell and the sure knowledge that everything was going to be just the same tomorrow – Noah picked up his best pencil and squeezed it so tight that it snapped in his hands. 'I have to *decide*,' he thought.

Then, in the exact moment that the clock struck 3.15 p.m. and the bell rang for the end of school, Noah made a decision instead of a wish.

"I need more of me," he said.

Chapter 3
Another Noah

Wednesday.

Noah awoke at 06.45 a.m. as normal and ate his breakfast.

- 1 dippy egg boiled for five minutes as normal.

- 1 slice of white toast buttered to the edges as normal.

- 1 tall glass of cold milk drunk with a straw as normal.

Then Noah began the walk to school. It took nine minutes. On the way, he made a list in his head of as many dinosaurs as he could remember.

So far, so Wednesday.

It was only when Noah arrived at his classroom that things changed. Someone was sitting in his chair.

Noah blinked, two times.

No, it was not *someone* sitting in his chair.

It was him.

He was sitting in his chair.

Dundlewick Doubling – Day 1
Number Of Noahs – 2

This other Noah was identical to him in every way. He had Noah's dark, curly hair that looked untidy no matter how much Noah brushed it. He had Noah's upturned nose ... he had his chipped front tooth. It was like looking in a mirror, except the Noah that Noah saw did not look like a mirror image. This other Noah was 100% absolutely the same as he was!

"Whuh?" was all Noah could say.

The other Noah looked at him. By now the rest of the class had seen that there were two Noahs. A few of them shrank back to the corners of the classroom. Some peered at the pair, fascinated. Others scowled with suspicion.

Noah ignored them all. He walked slowly towards the other Noah, his heart thumping in his chest.

"You ... you're another me," Noah said at last, his eyes wide. "Did – did I *decide* you?"

"Well, I didn't decide you, so I suppose you decided me," the other Noah said with a shrug. "Now here I am."

"It worked … my not-wishing worked!" Noah laughed. He looked his double up and down. "All that time I spent wishing … I should have known it was a waste of time. I just needed to *decide*."

"Looks like it!" the other Noah said. "So, how many different dinosaur names did you think of on the way to school today?"

"One hundred and two," Noah said.

"Three more than yesterday," the other Noah said.

"Wait, how do you know how many dinosaurs I counted yesterday, but not how many I counted today?" Noah asked.

"You know as much as I do," the other Noah said. "Maybe we're just a *little* bit different. But other than that –"

"We're the same," they said together.

A grin spread across the faces of both Noahs, but Noah's grin was just a little bit bigger. This was *his* doing, after all. He had decided this.

"Morning, Owl Class," said Miss Fiddy in a jolly-for-a-Wednesday voice. She skipped into the classroom with her arms full of exercise books. "And how is Owl Class doing tod-aAAAH!"

Miss Fiddy dropped the exercise books as she stared at the two Noahs. "Two!" she blurted in horror. "How two? Who how? Two who ..."

"You sound like an owl, Miss," both Noahs said together.

Noah watched as his teacher tried to work it out.

It was clear to Miss Fiddy that the other Noah wasn't an identical twin. Twins may look the same but they move differently and breathe differently and think differently. They *are* different. These two Noahs were the same person – almost 100% the very same human being. Noah had been exactly doubled down to every last untidy hair on his head.

"It's OK, Miss, I'll get a spare chair from the back," Noah said. "Noah and I can share."

And that was that. For the rest of the day, Owl Class had two Noahs.

Chapter 4
Noah and the Other Noah

Noah and the other Noah hit it off right away.
After all, they had a lot in common.

They agreed on the simple joy of a glass
of ice-cold milk. They agreed on the delicious
taste of a plate of spaghetti and tomato sauce.

And, of course, they agreed that there was
nothing in the world more important than
dinosaurs. In fact, they had *everything* in
common, down to the very last thought. They
knew what the other one was thinking, and
had just thought, and was about to think, which

meant that conversations between the two Noahs tended to go like this.

"The best thing about the *spinosaurus* is –"

"Totally."

"Do you think the *ankylosaurus* –"

"Definitely."

"I bet the *parasaurolophus* never –"

"Of course not!"

After the first couple of hours, the two Noahs could tell each other everything with a look ... and soon they worked out they didn't even need to do that. They didn't say another thing to each other on their first day together. Noah didn't mind at all. At last, he had found someone who agreed with him on everything.

At lunch time, the two Noahs stood together in the queue.

"Before you ask, Noah, *no* – there is no spaghetti and tomato sauce," Mrs Tuckin said, as Noah reached the front of the lunch queue. "Today is pizza. Still, at least it's still … Italian …"

Mrs Tuckin fell silent as the other Noah stepped out from behind his double. Mrs Tuckin, who had seen a lot of odd things in her time, stared hard at the two Noahs but kept her cool.

"What's all this then?" she asked.

"I decided I needed more of me," Noah said.

"So here I am," the other Noah said.

"You said I can't always get what I want, but I might get what I need," Noah added with a grin. "But now there's two of me, so I have what I want *and* what I need."

"For the record, Noah, I did *not* mean for you to double yourself." Mrs Tuckin tutted, as she waved her spatula at them. "Anyway, I haven't time for hocus-pocus – hold out your plates."

The Noahs looked down at their empty plates, then at the hot, fresh pizza.

"We want spaghetti and tomato sauce," they said together.

Mrs Tuckin let out a sigh.

"Catilla the Hun did a poo in my fruit bowl *and* my slippers this morning, so I am in no mood for your usual objections," Mrs Tuckin said. She picked up another spatula and slapped a pizza slice on to both plates. "Now, if you look behind you, you'll find a hundred children who do want pizza, and I need to serve them too. *Arrivederci!* Farewell!"

Noah and the other Noah stared at their pizza slices. They pushed them around their plates with identical jabs of their fingers. Then, in the very same moment, they made a decision. They looked up together and stared at each other.

"We need more of us," they said.

Chapter 5
More Noahs

The Noahs did not have a good night's sleep.

Noah's mum and dad didn't sleep well either. They were altogether disturbed by the fact there were two of Noah. They spent all night on the internet looking for answers, and kept saying things like "How?" and "Impossible!" and "What will the neighbours say!"

They treated the doubling of Noah as if it was some sort of awful illness.

"It's OK. I just decided I needed more of me, that's all," Noah told his parents, but no one seemed to think that the doubling was a good idea – except for Noah and the other Noah ...

... Oh, and the two new Noahs that they found in the classroom the next morning.

Dundlewick Doubling – Day 2
Number Of Noahs – 4

"More of me!" Noah shouted when he saw the third and fourth Noahs. "We decided you! We decided you and now you're here!"

"We knew you were going to say that!" Noahs three and four laughed. They looked exactly the same as the other Noahs – doubles down to every tiny last detail.

"How many dinosaur names did you think of on the way to school?" the two new Noahs asked together.

"One hundred and six," Noah said.

"It would have been one hundred and five, but Noah saw a mouse and then he remembered *mosasaurus*," the second Noah said. "I hadn't thought of a *mosasaurus*."

"Maybe we're just a little bit different," Noah said.

The Noahs looked at each other, and then they both shrugged at the same time.

"Morning, Owl Class," Miss Fiddy said, in her only-two-more-days-to-the-weekend Thursday voice. She rushed into the room with a heap of exercise books in her arms, as normal. "How is Owl Class doing tod-aAAAAH!"

The exercise books fell to the floor with a KRU-DUMP! and Miss Fiddy went weak at the knees. If she hadn't held on to her desk she would have fallen to the ground in a heap.

"Four!" she blurted. "Two ... now more! More ... four!"

"It's OK, Miss, we'll find some spare chairs," Noah said. "We can share."

The four Noahs spent the morning huddled around a single desk, but it was clear that they needed more space. In the end, Miss Fiddy borrowed a table from another room and squeezed it into Owl Class. Everyone else had to shuffle back so that the new Noahs could fit.

The best thing about there being more Noahs was they had the chance to talk about dinosaurs in their lesson.

"Uh, who can give me an example of a verb?" Miss Fiddy asked.

"Eat!" Noah shouted out.

"And ... and would someone else like to use that verb in a sentence?" Miss Fiddy asked, ever hopeful.

"The *ceratosaurus* wants to EAT the *stegosaurus*!" the second Noah said.

"The *torvosaurus* couldn't EAT the *ceoplophysis* ..." the third Noah began.

"... Because the *ceoplophysis* didn't exist in the Jurassic period!" the fourth Noah added.

The four Noahs were proud of their verbs and of their dinosaur jokes ... but all the other children groaned. Miss Fiddy did her best to move the lesson on to something other than dinosaurs.

'Imagine if there were even more of me,' Noah thought. 'Imagine if there were more of me than everyone else ...'

Mrs Tuckin still didn't give them spaghetti and tomato sauce instead of chicken for lunch – even though all four Noahs asked for it.

By the end of the day, Noah was sure that the doubling had to go on. At the 3.15 p.m. bell, the four Noahs looked each other in the eye and decided.

"More," they said. "We still need *more*."

Chapter 6
Miss Fiddy Faints

On Friday morning, the four Noahs ate their dippy eggs and their white toast buttered to the edges, drank their glasses of cold milk and off they went to school. Their mum and dad waved them off weakly. They were even more disturbed by the *double* doubling of their Noah.

But all that the boys could think of was what was waiting for them in the classroom. Could there be more of them?

They were half way to school when they saw a woman run across the road towards them. She had wild brown hair and a cardigan that was so long and stretched it looked more like a cape.

"Boys! Boys!" the woman shouted. "I'm Anne Finally, *Dundlewick Herald*! Could I have a moment of your time?"

The four Noahs froze. They were not fans of strangers, and this lady looked like nothing but trouble.

"Is it true that two days ago there was only one of you?" Anne Finally went on. She took a notebook out of a pocket on her cardigan and pulled a pen out of her hair. "What's the story, boys? Are you long lost quadruplets? Were three of you kept in a cupboard against your will? Would you care to comment?"

It seemed that the news had got around about the doubling of the Noahs.

The Noahs weren't sure what to say, so they walked on and tried to pretend Anne Finally wasn't there.

But Anne chased after them, pen and notebook in hand. "Is it plastic surgery? Or are you clones made by mad scientists? The people of Dundlewick have a right to know!"

In the end, the Noahs decided to make a run for it. In silent agreement they started to race down the road. They didn't stop until they'd made it inside the school gates. As they dashed down the corridor towards their classroom, they spotted Miss Fiddy, her arms as full of books as ever.

"Don't run, Noah Noahs," she said, as she turned the corner into the classroom. "You know what they say, it's better to be late in this life than early in the next – AAAH!"

The Noahs heard a THUD-UMP!

Then a THUD.

The boys hurried into classroom to see Miss Fiddy flat out on the floor, her books all around her. She'd fainted. Noah knew why even before he looked up.

There were four more Noahs waiting for him.

"Yes! More!" Noah said aloud, pointing at the new Noahs. But right away, he decided they still needed more. Then, as if thinking Noah's own thoughts, the other seven called out, "More. We want more!"

"Then it's decided," Noah said with a grin. "More, more, more!"

Chapter 7
What a Difference a Weekend Makes

The eight Noahs woke up at 06.45 on Saturday morning as normal. They'd been crammed into Noah's house on blankets and sleeping bags and pillows. They were all over Noah's bedroom and most of the living room too.

"OK, let's –" Noah began, but before he could finish, the other seven Noahs said,

"Yes, let's!"

All the Noahs had come up with the same plan without saying a single word about it. After breakfast, even though it was Saturday, they would go to school and sneak into their classroom to see if more Noahs were waiting for them there.

But when Noah peered out of his bedroom window, he saw eight brand-new Noahs in the front garden. It seemed as if his doubles turned up wherever was best for them.

Dundlewick Doubling – Day 4
Number Of Noahs – 16

After an excellent day of pretending to be dinosaurs – in which all the Noahs pretended to be a *tyrannosaurus* – the 16 Noahs silently agreed that they needed yet more of them. They went to bed sure that they would double again ... and double they did.

On Sunday, 16 more Noahs turned up at the front door, adding to the 16 who were watching *Jurassic Park* in the living room.

Dundlewick Doubling – Day 5
Number Of Noahs – 32

So, when Monday rolled around, it was safe to say that Noah wasn't *very* surprised to find another 32 Noahs waiting for him in his classroom.

Dundlewick Doubling – Day 6
Number Of Noahs – 64

64 Noahs! That was more than double the number of other children in the class.

*

"I – I can't do this … I can't …!" Miss Fiddy sniffed as she arrived at the classroom door.

This time she flung all the exercise books to the floor – that is, the only bit of floor left uncovered. Noahs filled almost every inch of space, and the other children were pushed to the sides of the room.

"We can't even … where are you all … where am I going to … I can't do this!" Miss Fiddy sobbed.

In the end, Miss Fiddy took her class to the hall. The 64 Noahs sat on gym mats, while the other children sat behind them on the floor and waited to see what would happen next. Miss Fiddy, keen to start the lesson, stood at the front of the hall and looked at all the Noahs.

But whatever lesson Miss Fiddy had in mind for Monday morning, the 64 Noahs had their own ideas.

Chapter 8
You Can't Always Get What You Want

"Can – can anyone think of an example of a *palindrome?*" Miss Fiddy asked, as stressed as ever. "A palindrome is a word that is spelled the same both forwards and backwards, like 'deed' or 'noon'. Can anyone think of –"

All the Noahs put up their hands at once.

"N-Noah?" Miss Fiddy asked.

"*Dinosaur,*" Noah said. The word seemed to crack as it came out of his mouth. It was the first word he'd spoken in two days. Because all the Noahs shared the same thoughts and ideas, they almost never needed to talk to one another.

"Um, Noah, the word 'dinosaur' isn't spelled the same forwards and backwards, is it?" Miss Fiddy said. "You see –"

"But we want to learn about dinosaurs," said Noah.

"We all want to learn about dinosaurs," said another Noah.

"All of us," all 64 Noahs said together. The sound boomed around the hall.

"It – it doesn't work like that, Noah," Miss Fiddy said. "This is school. We can't learn about something just because you want to … and I mean, there are other children here that –"

"Dinosaurs!" the 64 Noahs chanted together. "DINOSAURS! DINOSAURS! DINOSAURS!"

It was all too much for Miss Fiddy. She ran out of the room with tears in her eyes.

"It serves her right," Noah said to himself, remembering all the times his teacher had stopped him talking about dinosaurs. But he felt a knot of guilt twist deep in the pit of his stomach.

Then Noah remembered it was Monday, and he forgot about everything except spaghetti and tomato sauce.

*

By the time it was lunch time, Noah somehow ended up at the end of the lunch queue behind the 63 other Noahs. He was happy to wait his turn – *nothing* was going to spoil Spaghetti Monday. He saw Mrs Tuckin handing plates full of hot spaghetti and tomato sauce to all his doubles and his mouth began to water.

"Spaghetti and tomato sauce, please," Noah said when he got to the front of the queue.

Mrs Tuckin waved her big spoon over the empty tray. "I've just run out," she said.

"Run out?" Noah said. "But it's Spaghetti Monday – I want spaghetti and tomato sauce."

"And I want a cat that knows the difference between a slipper and a litter tray," Mrs Tuckin said. "The fact is, there's too many of you, Noah. The spaghetti – like my dream of being an opera singer – is no more. I've had to cook up some of tomorrow's meat pie instead."

"Meat pie? But I don't want meat pie, I want spaghetti and tomato sauce!" Noah yelled. He pointed at all the other Noahs in the dining hall. "You can't give *them* spaghetti and tomato sauce and not me! I'm the first one! I'm the first me!"

"Is that so?" Mrs Tuckin said, giving him a sharp look. "How many of you are there now, by the way?"

"Sixty-four," Noah said. "So far."

"Well, that seems like plenty to me … maybe enough is enough," Mrs Tuckin said. She took a tray out of the oven and put it down in front of Noah. "Now, do you want some meat pie or not?"

Noah scowled. "What's in it?" he asked.

A smile flashed across Mrs Tuckin's face. "Meat," she said.

Chapter 9
Enough Is (Not) Enough

After he was forced to eat meat pie on a Monday, Noah decided that maybe it was time to take a break from doubling. Not because Mrs Tuckin said so – he didn't have to do what she told him! But maybe, just maybe, 64 Noahs *was* enough. After all, they made up nearly a third of all the children at school.

Noah felt the need to tell the other Noahs what he thought – even though he was sure they must be thinking the very same as him.

"I've decided we should stop deciding," Noah declared, as he and the other Noahs walked home. "I mean, the house is full and Mum and Dad said we'll need to move ... and Mrs Tuckin ran out of spaghetti and tomato sauce at lunch time. There are too many of us now ... maybe we need to decide *not* to make more of us."

"No more?" a Noah asked. He sounded a little surprised.

"No more," Noah said. "OK?"

None of the Noahs said anything and, for the first time ever, Noah wasn't sure exactly what the other Noahs were thinking.

"I mean, at least we should wait for a few days," Noah added. "Then, if we do decide we need more of us, we can decide to start again."

"Then ... it's decided," three of the Noahs said together.

Noah breathed a small sigh of relief. Then he saw the other Noahs flash a look at one another that he didn't understand at all.

*

On Tuesday morning, Noah raced ahead of the other Noahs as they made their way to school. He had to be sure the doubling had stopped ... for now, at least. He was almost at the school gates when he heard his name ring out.

"Noah! Noah Scape!"

Noah turned to see the reporter, Anne Finally, sprinting down the street after him, her hair as wild as ever. "It is Noah, isn't it?" she asked.

"I have to go to school!" Noah shouted, racing on.

But Anne Finally chased after him, notebook in hand and cardigan flapping.

"People are calling it the 'Dundlewick Doubling'! Rumour has it you boys are doubling daily!" she said as she ran past Noah. Then she spun around and blocked his path just before he got to the school gates. "In another week there'll be thousands of you, Noah!"

"I don't know what you're – Wait, *thousands*?" Noah blurted.

"It's true, isn't it?" Anne Finally said. "You've been doubling your numbers every day for more than a week now. First two, then four, then eight …" She took out her notebook. "I did the maths – do you want to see?"

'The maths?' Noah thought.

And all of a sudden he wondered why he hadn't worked out the maths himself. Anne Finally was right – the Noahs were indeed doubling their numbers every day – and that number was going to get very big, very fast. Anne Finally opened her notebook, and held it OUT to show Noah.

The words 'DUNDLEWICK DOUBLING?!?' were written at the top of the page and under them –

Day 1 – (2)

Day 2 – (4)

Day 5 – (32)

Day 10 – (1,024)

Day 12 – (4,096)

Day 15 – (32,768)

Day 20 – (1,048,576)

Day 30 – (1,073,741,824) !!!!

Noah gulped, hard.

"Thirty days? Isn't that, like, a month?"
he muttered. Anne Finally nodded and Noah
peered at the notebook. "How big is – how
many is that big number?"

"One billion, seventy-three million, seven
hundred and forty-one thousand, eight hundred
and twenty-four Noahs ... in one month," Anne
Finally said.

Noah felt sick. He couldn't even picture
a *billion* of him, or a billion of anyone or
anything for that matter. Was there even
enough spaghetti and tomato sauce in the
whole world to feed that many Noahs?

"Wait, it's OK," he said, remembering what
he'd decided yesterday. He looked back and
pointed at the 63 Noahs walking up the street
towards them. "I – we – decided. We decided
we needed to stop making more of me."

"You did?" Anne Finally said. She turned around and looked at the school. "Then, who are they?"

From out of the front doors came more Noahs. They walked out into the playground, one after the other ... all 64 of them. The Noahs had doubled again.

Dundlewick Doubling – Day 7
Number Of Noahs – 128

"More? But – but I decided!" Noah said. "I decided we needed to stop!"

"We decided something else," said one of the Noahs from behind him.

"But – but you're me! You're all me! We decided the same thing!" Noah cried.

"Maybe we're a little bit different," another Noah said. "Either way, we decided that you don't get to decide."

"Yeah, we decided we're not going to stop," another Noah added. "Not now, not *ever*."

Chapter 10
You Might Get What You Need

Dundlewick Doubling – Day 8
Number Of Noahs – 256

It had been eight days since Noah Scape first decided he needed more of him. There were now more Noahs than any other children at school. The head teacher said they would have to move the whole school to a huge warehouse outside Dundlewick. But Noah knew that in two more days a warehouse wouldn't be big enough. In fact, if Anne Finally was right, in a month's time even the whole *country* wouldn't be big enough.

That Wednesday morning, Miss Fiddy took her class into the hall again. There were 256 Noahs and 23 other children in Owl Class.

Miss Fiddy spent the morning teaching her class about dinosaurs.

The Noahs listened to every word Miss Fiddy said, happy that they already knew everything about dinosaurs. But Noah wasn't listening at all. Instead, he stared out of the window at an enormous truck as it drove into the school gates. When it stopped, the drivers got out and unloaded crate after massive crate. Some crates were marked SPAGHETTI and some crates were marked TOMATO SAUCE.

'Spaghetti and tomato sauce on a Wednesday?' Noah thought. Even Mrs Tuckin, it seemed, had to adapt to this new way of life. 'Looks like it's going to be spaghetti and tomato sauce every day from now on,' Noah thought.

So when Noah found himself last in the queue for lunch, he didn't worry – he knew there would be plenty of his favourite food to go around …

But, for once, he wasn't sure he wanted it.

"Last in the queue … but you're the first, aren't you?" Mrs Tuckin said, as she put another tray of hot, fresh spaghetti and tomato sauce in front of him. She wiped sweat from her brow. "I mean, you're the first Noah. You're the original one. There's something different about you, I can tell."

"How?" Noah asked.

"Because all those other Noahs look like they got what they want, but not you," Mrs Tuckin said. "Still, like the song goes, *if you try, sometimes you might get what you need.*"

"I still don't know what that means," Noah confessed.

Mrs Tuckin shrugged. She scooped up a big new spoon of spaghetti and held it out, but Noah pulled his plate away.

"Do ... do you have meat pie?" he asked.

*

As it turned out, Mrs Tuckin had baked some pie just for the children who weren't Noahs. She gave the last of it to Noah. He still wasn't a big fan of meat pie, but he did enjoy the fact that it wasn't spaghetti and tomato sauce.

After lunch, Noah made his way outside to the playground. There were Noahs as far as the eye could see. In fact, Noah hadn't seen anyone *except* other Noahs all day. Where were the other children? Where was the rest of Owl Class?

Noah went back inside. They had to be somewhere. Where had they all gone?

Noah walked around the school, looking for anyone who didn't look exactly like him. Since the Noahs were so silent, the school was silent too. There was only the echo of the Noahs' identical footsteps around the corridors.

At last, Noah came to the school library. He hadn't been in there for a week, since both the books about dinosaurs had been taken out by other Noahs. He peered in the window in the door. The rest of his class was there, reading, talking or playing games.

Noah stared. There were so many different faces and names and games. He could hear the hum of chat, jokes and laughter – laughter! Noah hadn't heard laughter all week. He realised that he'd missed it.

Noah took a deep breath and walked into the library.

Everyone froze.

"Sorry," he said, but he didn't know why.

"We don't want to play 'dinosaurs'," one boy said.

"Or talk about dinosaurs, or read about dinosaurs, or do anything else about dinosaurs," one of the girls added.

"I – I know," Noah said. "I don't want to either. I just thought – I just wondered if ... if I could play whatever *you're* playing?"

To Noah's surprise, the other children let him join in. For the first time in ages, Noah played with someone who wasn't his identical double ... and none of the games were dinosaur games. Noah rarely talked with the other Noahs, so he'd got used to being quiet. Instead, he listened.

Noah listened to the other children's thoughts and ideas, and he found out things he never knew. He found out that pigs can't look

up, and that Venus is the only planet in the solar system that rotates clockwise, and that, however hard you try, you can't lick your own elbow.

Noah spent the afternoon in the library with the other children. Everyone was different, but that made Noah feel like himself again. He finally understood what Mrs Tuckin meant – this might not have been what he wanted, but it was exactly what he needed.

Of course, in the back of his mind, Noah knew that tomorrow the number of Noahs would double again. And the next day, and the next, until there were thousands … millions … billions of Noahs.

But, for the moment, Noah just played.

Our books are tested
for children and young people by
children and young people.

Thanks to everyone who consulted on
a manuscript for their time and effort in
helping us to make our books better
for our readers.